The Car Wash

By Maggie van Galen and Dr. Amy Wheadon, OTD, OTR/L

Illustrations by Leslie Beauregard

King's Day Out–The Car Wash
All Rights Reserved.
Copyright ©2020 Maggie van Galen and Dr. Amy Wheadon, OTD, OTR/L
King's Day Out LLC
www.KingsDayOut.com

Illustrations by Leslie Beauregard

Graphic design and layout by Little Bridge Design
Pet photography by Pant The Town Photography (www.pantthetown.com)

Pear Tree Publishing
www.peartreepublishing.net

First Edition

Printed by Ingram Spark

ISBN 978-1-62502-024-6
Library of Congress Number: 2020921743

PUBLISHED IN THE UNITED STATES OF AMERICA

This book is dedicated to my sons, Luke and Dylan, for convincing us to bring, Koning (Dutch for King), the sweetest puppy ever, into our family; and to my dear friend, Rachel, for giving me the idea for this book!

Always Follow Your Dreams!

Maggie

This book is dedicated to my three children, Lily, Jack and Madison, who have supported me in my dream to create an OT practice that helps so many children; and to all the amazing, intuitive children with sensory differences who work hard every day to unlock their potential and learn to navigate their worlds with success.

Strong Bodies. Strong Minds. Strong Hearts. And Helping Kids SHINE!

Amy

A message to parents & caregivers:

Every child has their own unique way of viewing and interacting with the world, and that includes individualized responses to sensory information. As a pediatric occupational therapist for over 20 years, I have worked with countless children who are incredibly smart, vibrant, and endearing, and who have difficulty participating in daily activities due to challenges processing and responding to sensory information in their environment. Along with helping children with sensory processing challenges to self regulate, OTs provide tools and strategies for self awareness, self advocacy and task success.

The **King's Day Out** book series is designed to be a resource for children, families, schools and pediatric medical professionals. These books will provide concrete examples of common tools that OTs may recommend to support a particular child at home, in the classroom and in the world. I firmly believe that once a child is able to recognize which stimuli causes a particular reaction, what that reaction is, and what tool can be used, the more successful that child will be in his or her daily occupations.

Sincerely,

Dr. Amy Wheadon, OTD, OTR/L

Please visit **www.KingsDayOut.com** for more resources.

2

A message to the kiddos:

Hi kids!

I want to introduce you to a puppy named King and his best friend; a boy named Ben. King loves Ben very much! Ben and King both have a lot of energy and sometimes get nervous about new adventures, which can make it hard to stay calm and focused.

Ben has been working really hard with his occupational therapist (OT) who helps him to understand what his body is thinking and feeling. He has a special "adventure bag" filled with tools. These tools help Ben's body have a "just right engine" and help him focus both at home and at school, allowing him to feel calm and safe. Ben shares these special tools with his puppy friend, King, so they can both have a positive experience on their latest adventure to *The Car Wash*!

Enjoy the ride!
Dr. Amy

My name is King, and I am a Bernese Mountain Dog puppy.

I have lots of energy and like to run, play with my toys, and dig in the garden. My best friend is a boy named Ben.

Ben and I go on lots of adventures together.

Today we are going to the car wash.

Before we leave, Mom goes through our routine. She takes off my house collar and puts on my travel collar. Then she helps Ben put on his shoes and socks and reminds him to grab his adventure bag. Ben says the tools inside help him with situations that might make him nervous. He shows me how to use them and they really work!

Ben and I have never been to the car wash before. Mom tells us a story about one so we will know what to expect. She says the car will go into a special garage to wash off the dirt. It will be dark, like a tunnel, and we won't be able to see out of the windows because of the water, colorful soap, and scrubbers. She says there will be new smells and loud noises but that nothing will come inside the car because all the windows will be closed. Then Mom shows us pictures of a car wash and our schedule for the day.

My tummy starts to have butterflies like it does when I eat kibble too fast.

Mom says we can go to the park after the car wash. Ben and I love the park! Sometimes Ben swings on the swing set while Mom and I play ball, then I take a nap and Ben draws in his notebook.

On the way to the car wash, Mom rolls down my window so I can stick my head out and feel the air on my face. It's so much fun! My ears flap back, and I feel like a race dog! Ben keeps his window up, but he likes watching me with my face in the wind.

The car slows down. Ben and I see the long garage Mom told us about. When we drive in, a man greets Mom at her window. He waves to Ben and pats me on the head. I love getting pats!

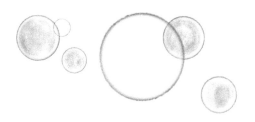

"Okay boys," Mom says, "windows up! Here we go! Remember, first you will see soap bubbles on the windows. Nothing will come inside, but you may be able to smell the soap."

Ben takes my paw.

spurt squirt spurt squirt spurt squirt

Blue and pink foam squirts onto the front of the car, drips down the sides, covers the windows, and then splashes over the back. I hop back and forth between the front and back seats, barking and chasing the bubbles. It smells like flowers. This is fun! I am getting really excited!

Now I can hear something loud. Ben starts squirming and twisting his seat belt, so I know he hears it too and is getting nervous, just like me. I climb back into the seat next to Ben.

"Don't worry, King. I'm here," Ben says, giving me a big, tight hug.

I love hugs like this! They make me feel so safe and calm.

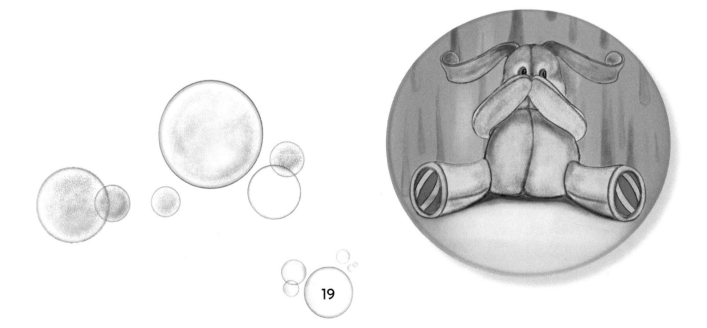

"The noises you hear are the scrubbers," Mom explains. "It looks like the arms of a big blue octopus dangling down. They will spin and mix all of the soap on the outside of the car."

She isn't joking! Blue whirling arms slap the windows. They look like they are coming from everywhere.

swish splat swish splat swish splat

Ben and I don't like this part of the car wash. He reaches into his adventure bag, pulls out his heavy blanket, and lays it over us. The blanket is heavier than anything I've ever felt. It's like having a whole-body hug! I snuggle in closer to Ben. He talks softly to me and pets my head. With Ben next to me, I know it will be okay, but I like the bubbles better.

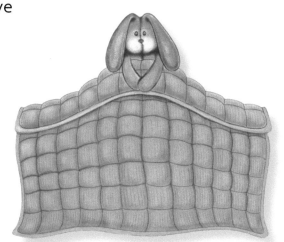

"Two more steps—rinse and dry—and then we're done!" Mom says in her gentle tone. "Rinse is like rain. Water sprays down to rinse off the soap."

I like rain! At home I get all muddy and wet stomping in the puddles. When I come inside, Ben calls me a "soggy doggy" and we play tug of war with my towel. Maybe this part of the car wash will be better.

Here comes the rain! I see it hit the hood of the car. That's a lot of water!

I peek to see the water running down the windows and rinsing the bubbles away. We're not getting wet at all. This car wash thing is pretty cool!

Sploosh Splash Sploosh Splash
Sploosh Splash

23

"Cover your ears for this last part," Mom says gently. "This is the dryer, and it's very noisy. There are big fans that blow air over the car. Just like the soap and water, we won't feel it inside the car."

The fans are louder than Mom's hairdryer!

whoosh whir whoosh whir whoosh whir

I scrunch down and bury my head under Ben's arm. Ben puts on his sound blocker headphones and covers my ears with his hands. This muffles the sounds and makes us feel better.

When I peek out, I see a light up ahead. We are at the end!
Mom turns and gives a high five to Ben and rubs behind my ears.
She tells us how awesome we are!

I'm tail-wagging happy that my friend Ben is on this adventure
with me. I'm so proud of us both. Now I know that next time we
go to the car wash, it will be okay!

Woof woof! It's time to go to the park!!

Adventure Time!

Time for an adventure of your own? Fun games for any age!

How many tennis balls can you find?	What name would you give Ben's bunny?	How many of King's paw prints do you see?

_____	_____	_____

Here are some of the tools* that Ben takes with him.

How many tools can you find?

  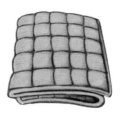

_____   _____   _____

What would you put in your adventure bag?
Draw some pictures of your favorite things to bring on an adventure!

About the Authors

MAGGIE VAN GALEN
www.maggievangalen.com

Maggie van Galen is an author, storyteller and writer and co-owner of King's Day Out LLC. Her previous works, *The Adventures of Keeno and Ernest* children's book series, have all received the nationally acclaimed Mom's Choice Awards. Maggie grew up in northern Michigan and has written from the time she was a young girl. She graduated from Michigan State University studying advertising, journalism and creative writing. After starting her family, the children's stories began to flow and her life as an author and storyteller began. Maggie lives in Georgetown, Massachusetts with her husband, two sons, a cat and their Bernese Mountain Dog, Koning (Dutch for King).

AMY WHEADON
www.kidshine-ot.com

Dr. Amy Wheadon is a pediatric occupational therapist and the owner of **kidSHINE LLC** in Rowley and Amesbury, MA and co-owner of King's Day Out LLC. She is also the creator and founder of the evidence based, *kidSHINE Bootcamp Program*®, a program that uses intense physical exercise to improve self-regulation in children with sensory processing challenges.

Amy grew up in Westchester County, New York. After graduating from Colby College, she completed her Master of Science in Occupational Therapy at Boston University and her doctorate in OT at NEIT. Over the past 20 years, Amy has worked as an occupational therapist in both public school systems and in outpatient pediatric clinics. Amy continues to merge her love of working with children with her passion for exercise and fitness at **kidSHINE LLC**.

Amy lives in Boxford, Massachusetts with her three children and their puppy, Luna.

About the Illustrator

LESLIE BEAUREGARD
www.lesliebeauregardart.com

Leslie Beauregard is a lover of "all things creative". The road to making art has taken many detours which has allowed her to focus on raising her family. When the opportunity to create again arrived, Leslie's drawings and paintings took on the purpose of telling narrative stories. Her journey as an illustrator was born. She hopes her artwork is engaging and makes people smile.

Leslie lives in Amesbury, Massachusetts with her husband, Jim and her rescue dog Skipper. She is a member of the Seacoast Artist Association, the Newburyport Art Association, the Greater Haverhill Art Association and a member of the Society of Children's Book Writers and Illustrators, and the Women's Business League.

CPSIA information can be obtained
at www.ICGtesting.com
Printed in the USA
BVHW020104141221
623981BV00002B/7